Mary and Victor
THEIR FIRST ADVENTURE

Copyright © 2022 Nara Farrell.

All rights reserved. No part of this book may be used or reproduced by any means, graphic, electronic, or mechanical, including photocopying, recording, taping or by any information storage retrieval system without the written permission of the author except in the case of brief quotations embodied in critical articles and reviews.

This is a work of fiction. All the characters, names, incidents, organizations, and dialogue in this novel are either the products of the author's imagination or are used fictitiously.

iUniverse books may be ordered through booksellers or by contacting:

iUniverse
1663 Liberty Drive
Bloomington, IN 47403
www.iuniverse.com
844-349-9409

Because of the dynamic nature of the internet, any web addresses or links contained in this book may have changed since publication and may no longer be valid. The views expressed in this work are solely those of the author and do not necessarily reflect the views of the publisher, and the publisher hereby disclaims any responsibility for them.

Any people depicted in stock imagery provided by Getty Images are models, and such images are being used for illustrative purposes only. Certain stock imagery © Getty Images.

ISBN: 978-1-6632-4038-5 (sc)
ISBN: 978-1-6632-4039-2 (e)

Library of Congress Control Number: 2022909905

Print information available on the last page.

iUniverse rev. date: 07/20/2022

A Note to The Readers

This book is based on stories recounted by Mary Dell. For four summers and winters, she and I spent days together walking, crafting, storytelling, and laughing. Mary was born in Ontario, Canada, in 1926. As a child, she would climb trees, walk miles across fields, and play with farm animals, living freely with nature. She recalled her adventures fondly and with pride and how animals made her feel secure and happy. She didn't have a class cat like the one in this book, but later on she did have a husband named Victor. They had quite a few adventures together!

Mary was brought up to believe that with imagination we find a certain freedom that will bring us to who we really are. By being herself, she taught me how to find myself, and I will always be grateful for her colourful ways. Her laughter fills my head as much as her stories do. This book is for her and the memories she shared about her family.

I would also like to acknowledge two other people who have supported the creation of this book.

A thank-you goes to Terra Sullivan for her magnificent illustrations. They are vibrant and really make the story pop! I am so lucky to know such a talented illustrator.

I am grateful to Cindy Dell, Mary Dell's daughter, for her contact when I was feeling rather helpless. Her friendship throughout has been a blessing.

And I thank everyone who reads this little book of ours. We hope you enjoy it and live your life to its fullest! Mary and Victor certainly did.

It's quite normal for a class cat to get all the attention. Children want to show off the fact that their class, out of all twelve classes in the school, has a mascot. Everyday Miss Cater brings Victor to school and the children take turns feeding and cleaning out his litter box, and every weeknight, Miss Cater takes him home with her. Everyone had had a turn taking Victor, the black cat, home for the weekend. Mary would be the last.

Mary was the type of girl who kept to herself. She didn't really have any close friends at school. She climbed trees and walked through fields for miles and miles, picking up sticks and any other interesting "treasures", as she called them. Deep down, she felt left out.

One day in class, Mary was using some of the tree bark she had found by gluing it onto her boat picture to make the sides look real. Mary's teacher, Miss Cater, came over to her, carrying Victor in her arms.

"That is beautiful, Mary. Your boat looks really good." She smiled down at Mary. "It's your turn to take Victor home for the weekend. Are you ready?"

Mary trembled with excitement! She was quite shy and usually held back her feelings, but not this time. She smiled a big, goofy grin, showing all her teeth. "Looks like you'll be having a very, very good weekend," her teacher said.

At the end of the school day, Miss Cater gave Victor and his cat supplies to Mary, saying, "You know what to do."

Mary did in fact know what to do. She had been listening when Miss Cater told the class how to care for Victor at home.

Mary loved animals and had wanted to be the last to take Victor home. She had remained silent when all the other children had their hands up, shouting, "Me! Me! I want to!" Mary didn't mind waiting and building up the excitement. It was her turn now. Oh yes!

That weekend, Mary and Victor did everything together. When Mary ate, Victor ate–at the table too. Mary's mum looked upset and started to say something. Then she seemed to change her mind. "Well, it's just for the weekend," she said. "So what's a little mess when you look so happy?"

Mary and Victor played in the barn together amongst the cows and the hay bales. Mary ran through the fields with Victor chasing her and fell down, laughing, quite out of breath. It was sunny and warm, and there was no end to the fun they had together.

But as Sunday came to an end, Mary started to feel sad. Soon she would have to give Victor back to the class, and their fun would be over. Her mum came into her room.

"Time for sleep, Mary and Victor." She laughed and kissed Mary on the forehead.

Then her dad came in. He gave Mary a hug and scratched Victor under his chin.

Victor even got to sleep on Mary's bed with her—another thing her mum let her do "just for the weekend". Mary and Victor drifted off to sleep and woke to the sound of Mum singing and cooking breakfast.

That morning Mary dreaded school. She walked very slowly into the classroom with Victor walking beside her.

As she and Victor walked into the classroom, they were greeted by her classmates, asking questions and patting her on the back.

"How did you get Victor to walk with you?"

"How did you do that?"

"That's amazing!"

Mary couldn't believe it! They'd hardly spoken with her before, and now they had lots of questions and seemed excited to hear what she said. Mary felt like a celebrity.

Mary hadn't actually thought about it. Victor learned to walk with her without Mary knowing she had done anything special. It just happened that way.

As they entered the classroom, her teacher smiled. When all her pupils had settled down, Miss Cater addressed them.

"Now class, since Mary was the last one to take Victor home, I want you all to draw a picture of your experience with Victor and put your names on the back."

The class got busy. Lots of pencils made scraping noises on paper. When it was all over, Miss Cater gathered up all the pictures and pinned them on the art wall. She stood back and observed the artwork, then smiled and said, "How interesting ..."

There were eleven black-and-white drawings and one in colour: eleven black cats, and one bursting with blues, reds, purples, and gold!

The children whispered amongst themselves.

"Who did the coloured one?"

"It's not right!"

"Victor is black!"

Miss Cater looked at the name on the back of the brightly coloured picture. Written very strongly in pencil was the name *Mary*.

Miss Cater looked at Mary again and smiled. She called Mary up to the front of the class.

"You see, children," she said, "not everything is black and white. Some imaginations are full of colour, just like Mary's."

Miss Cater smiled and looked back at the class.

"Now that we have all taken Victor home, we are going to start letting him play outside with us!"

The children were excited!

"And Mary, I can see that you and Victor have something special, why don't you help us with Victor outside? Teach us some things? Yes? We can start next week."

Mary nodded and looked at Victor, who was looking right back at her. She couldn't wait for next week!

CPSIA information can be obtained
at www.ICGtesting.com
Printed in the USA
BVHW020549011022
648433BV00003B/30